Monkey: Not ready for the baby

Marc Brown

Alfred A. Knopf   New York

Monkey is having a rough day.

And then it gets worse.

"I like being a little brother."

Mommy and Daddy say the new baby is coming SOON.

They talk about it a lot.

They read books about babies,

Here Comes Baby!

Baby Crawls.
Baby

They visit friends with babies.

"Does he cry
all the time?"

Suddenly, Monkey sees babies everywhere.
At the park.
At the store.
At school.

And soon there will be a baby in Monkey's house. He's not ready for that.

Monkey even dreams about babies.

Billions
of babies!

In the morning, Monkey draws a funny picture of the new baby flying far away into space.

Daddy finds photos of Monkey and his brother when they were babies.

"I was a cute baby."

"That's me giving you my fuzzy-wuzzy. That's when I became a big brother."

And mommy opens a box of their old baby clothes.

"This was your baby cup. Maybe the new baby would like it."

"I loved that cup. It's my cup."

Monkey wants to play with his friends, but instead he goes to the doctor with Mommy.

The doctor lets Monkey hear the baby's heartbeat.

"Put your hand here. You can feel the baby kick."

Mommy takes Monkey to Baby World.

Then he helps her pack her suitcase for the hospital.

Warm socks

snacks

camera

Money

skin lotion

cell phone and charger

makeup

shampoo

clothes for the new baby

a good book

The very next day, the baby is born—
and Monkey becomes a big brother.

"Look!
She opened her eyes!
Hello, my little sister."

☀ For Cora ☀
and her new brothers,
Leo and Julian

THIS IS A BORZOI BOOK PUBLISHED BY ALFRED A. KNOPF

Copyright © 2016 by Marc Brown

All rights reserved. Published in the United States by Alfred A. Knopf, an imprint of
Random House Children's Books, a division of Penguin Random House LLC, New York.

Knopf, Borzoi Books, and the colophon are registered trademarks of
Penguin Random House LLC.

Visit us on the Web! randomhousekids.com

Educators and librarians, for a variety of teaching tools, visit us at
RHTeachersLibrarians.com

Library of Congress Cataloging-in-Publication Data
Brown, Marc Tolon, author.
Monkey : not ready for the baby / Marc Brown. — First edition.
  pages cm.
Summary: Monkey is not ready to welcome a new baby to the family.
ISBN 978-1-101-93327-5 (trade) — ISBN 978-1-101-93328-2 (lib. bdg.) —
ISBN 978-1-101-93329-9 (ebook)
1. Monkeys—Juvenile fiction. 2. Infants—Juvenile fiction. 3. Brothers and sisters—
Juvenile fiction.
[1. Monkeys—Fiction. 2. Babies—Fiction. 3. Brothers and sisters—Fiction.] I. Title.
PZ7.B81618MI 2016
[E]—dc23
2015007135

The text of this book was created by hand by Marc Brown, accompanied by
a few typeset bits set in Elephant.
The illustrations were created using colored pencils and gouache.

MANUFACTURED IN CHINA
September 2016
10 9 8 7 6 5 4 3 2 1
First Edition